PEAS!

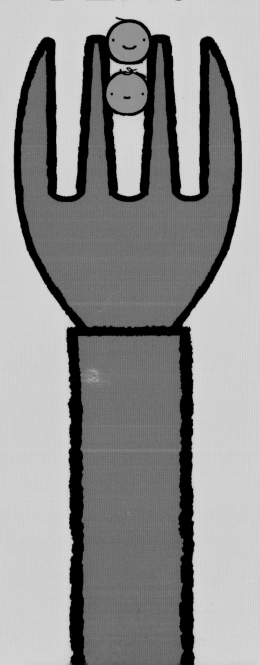

For Alice and Samuel – A.C.

For Mum, Dad and Erin Bean – S.R.

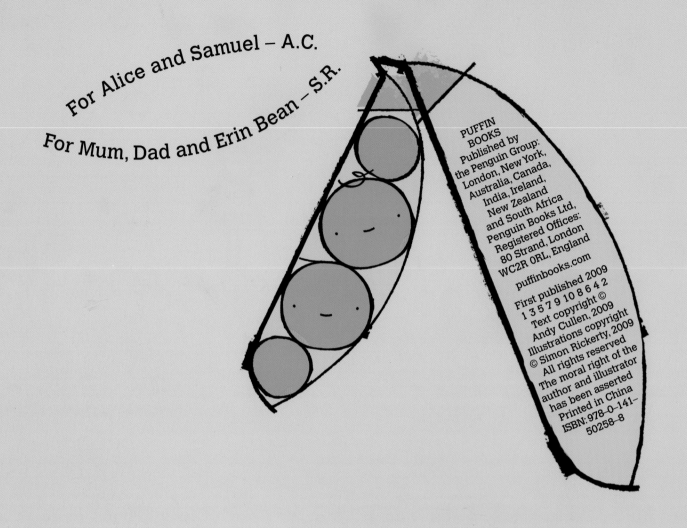

PUFFIN BOOKS
Published by the Penguin Group:
London, New York, Australia, Canada, India, Ireland, New Zealand and South Africa
Penguin Books Ltd, Registered Offices: 80 Strand, London WC2R 0RL, England

puffinbooks.com

First published 2009
1 3 5 7 9 10 8 6 4 2

Text copyright ©
Andy Cullen, 2009
Illustrations copyright
© Simon Rickerty, 2009

Printed in China
ISBN: 978-0-141-50258-8

PEAS!

IT'S NOT EASY BEING PEAS-Y

Andy Cullen and Simon Rickerty

PUFFIN

This is Pete.

This is **Penelope**.

This is their story . . .

A tractor **ploughs** the field.

A farmer takes a seed, and plants it in the ground.

Watered by the **rain**

warmed by the **sun**

the
peas
grOW

and

grOW

and

grOW.

The pods are **picked**

packed in a box

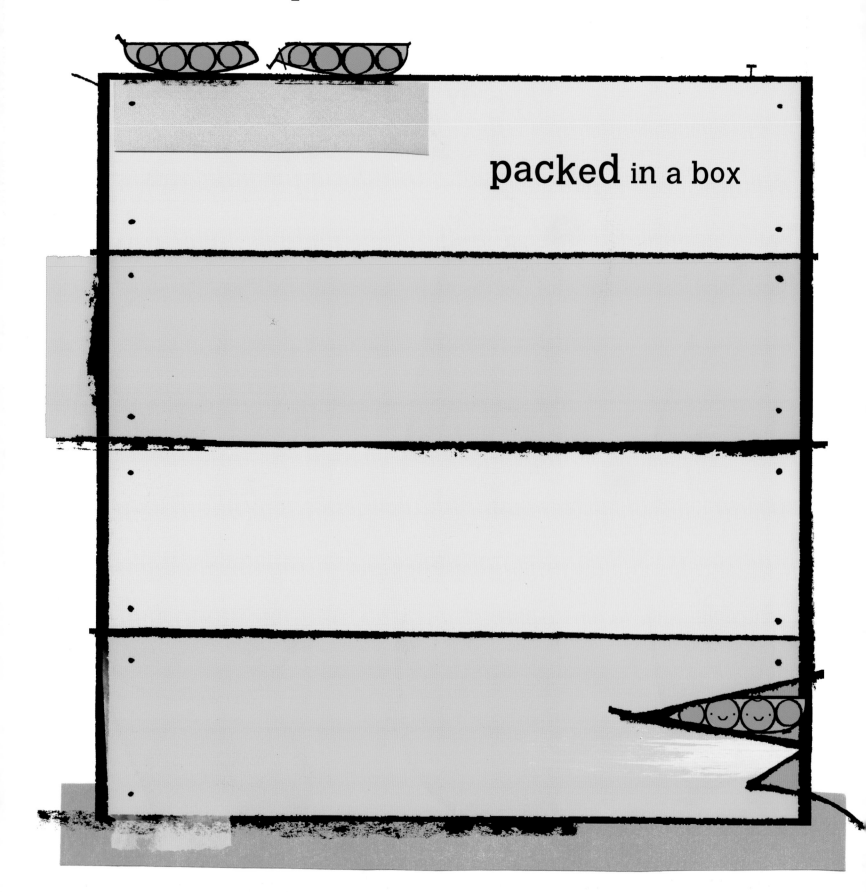

put on a truck and taken to
a pea factory.

Peas are **plucked** from the pods and **packed** in bags and tins.

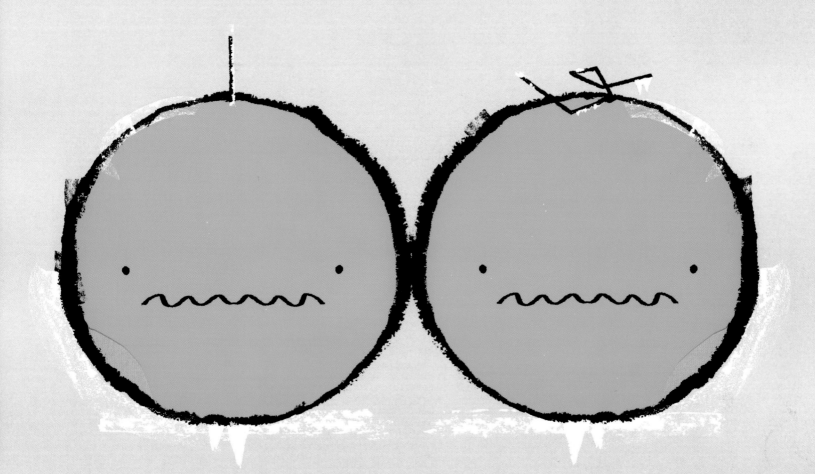

Some peas are **frozen**.

Peas travel all over planet earth—

on boats, on trains, on planes.

Peas live in shops.

Mummy and Daddy buy the peas,

take them home and **cook** them for supper.

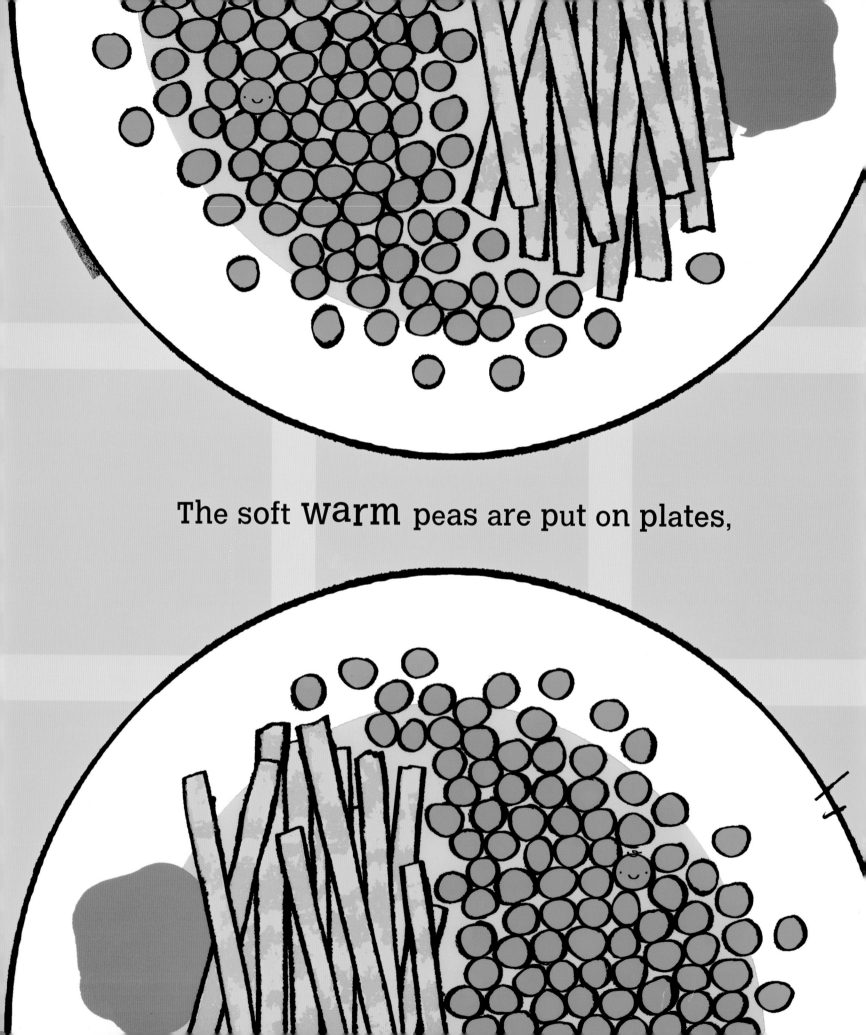

The soft warm peas are put on plates,

and given to the little princess
and the little prince.

The little princess says,

"I don't want peas!"

The little prince says,

"I don't want peas!"

"No!" say the peas.
"Try one, please!"

"Give peas a chance!"

Yum, yum . . .

WE ♡

PEAS!

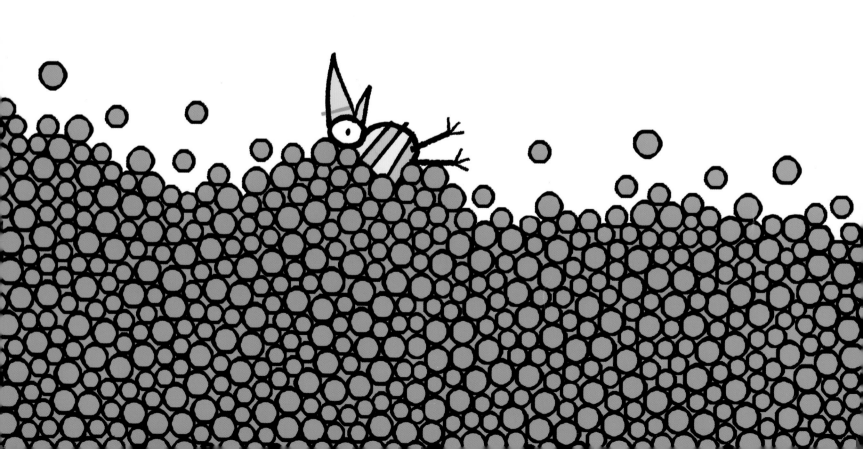

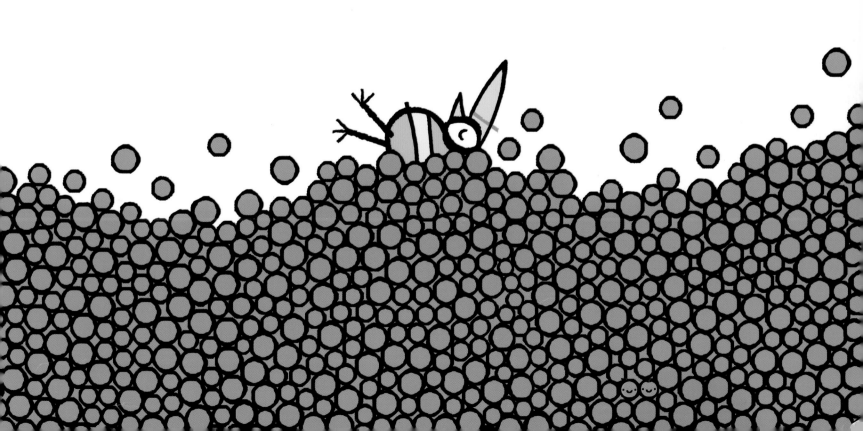